Withdrawn

D0466526

Shirley, Debra.
Best friend on wheels /

2008.
33305216489983
ca   10/20/08

BEST FRIEND ON WHEELS

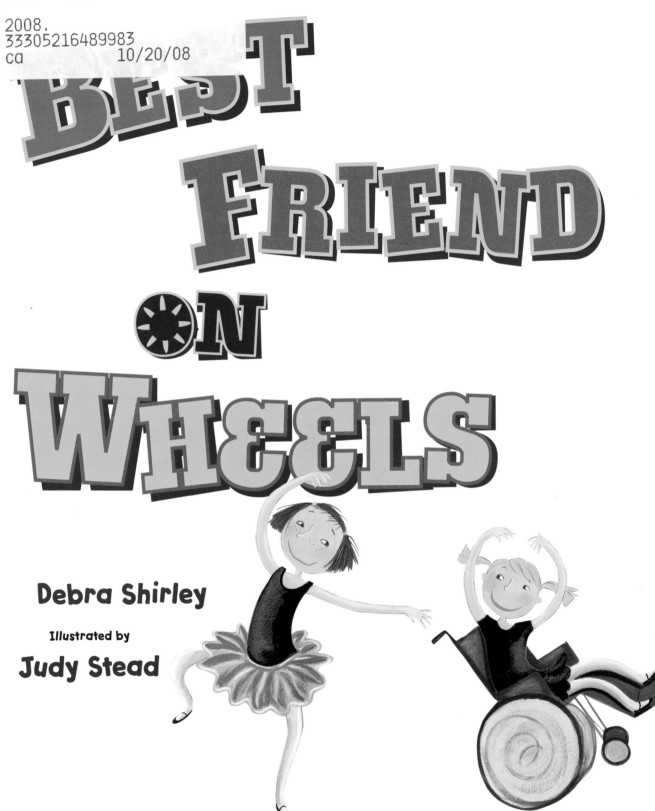

Debra Shirley

Illustrated by
Judy Stead

ALBERT WHITMAN & COMPANY, MORTON GROVE, ILLINOIS

For Gigi and Scott, and for my friends at Physically Handicapped
Actors and Musical Artists League (PHAMALy).—D.S.

To Zoe, who always has a best friend!—J.S.

Library of Congress Cataloging-in-Publication Data

Shirley, Debra.
Best friend on wheels / by Debra Shirley ; illustrated by Judy Stead.
p. cm.
Summary: A young girl relates all the ways she and her best friend, Sarah, are alike,
in spite of the fact that Sarah uses a wheelchair.
ISBN-13: 978-0-8075-8868-0 (hardcover)
[1. Best friends—Fiction. 2. Individuality—Fiction. 3. Friendship—Fiction. 4. Wheelchairs—Fiction. 5. People with
disabilities—Fiction. 6. Stories in rhyme.] I. Stead, Judy, ill. II. Title.
PZ8.3.S5569Be 2008 [E]—dc22 2007024252

Text copyright © 2008 by Debra Shirley.
Illustrations copyright © 2008 by Judy Stead.
Published in 2008 by Albert Whitman & Company,
6340 Oakton Street, Morton Grove, Illinois 60053-2723.
Published simultaneously in Canada by Fitzhenry & Whiteside, Markham, Ontario.
All rights reserved. No part of this book may be reproduced or transmitted in any form or by any means, electronic or
mechanical, including photocopying, recording, or by any information storage and retrieval system,
without permission in writing from the publisher.
Printed in the United States of America.
10 9 8 7 6 5 4 3 2 1

The design is by Carol Gildar.

For more information about Albert Whitman & Company,
visit our web site at www.albertwhitman.com.

Sarah, my best friend, is so much like me.
We like the same stuff and on *most* things agree.

We both like peach pie best. Our color is blue.
We both adore painting and reading, it's true!

We're both good at Frisbee. We like a good ballad.
We both pick the peppers off pizza and salad.

We're different in one way—she uses a wheelchair.

She rolls and I walk when we want to go somewhere.

We met when my second grade teacher, Miss Poole,
suggested I show "the new girl" around school.

"Sure! I'd be glad to! So, when do I meet her?"

"She's on her way now," said Miss Poole. "Let's go greet her."

When I saw she was using a wheelchair, I froze.
I fidgeted, twisted, and stared at my toes.

I was so nervous, I stammered and stuttered.
I might say the wrong thing, I thought—so I muttered.

I wanted to get a good look at her chair,
but I felt like a jerk, so I tried not to stare.

I looked all around till my eyes came to rest
on a shiny round button she wore on her vest.

ROCKHOUND it said, and I yelped with delight!
"Do you collect rocks?" And she grinned. "Yes, that's right!"

"So do I, I have crystals!" I practically squealed it.
"I've a rock tumbler," she said, and that sealed it.

The first time I stayed at her house overnight,
after movies, and popcorn, and a wild pillow fight,
it's hard to believe, but I actually said . . .

"I'd be happy to help get your wheelchair in bed!"

But Sarah said, "Silly, that's not how I do it!
I slide off my chair into bed—nothing to it!"

We ended up staying awake till midnight!
We hid under the covers and read by flashlight.

We told spooky stories until we got scared.
Then we each chose one page of our diaries and shared.

Ever since then we've been thicker than glue.
I've found out she does everything that *I* do.

We love making scrapbooks, we're great at cartooning.
Last summer we even went hot-air ballooning.

Dancing—yes, *dancing!* She loves the ballet.
She spins on her wheels and twirls every which way.

We're "peas in a pod," we hear everyone say.
We hang out together almost every day.

I mostly forget that we're different at all,
except once in a while, like today at the mall.

We stopped for an ice cream at quarter past three.
The ice cream clerk looked right past Sarah, to me.

The clerk was so nervous.
    She stammered.
    She stuttered.

"What flavor does *she* want?"
the clerk finally muttered.

She looked all around, till her eyes came to rest
on a shiny round button on Sarah's pink vest.

"I ♥ My Finches!" The clerk read the words.
"Finches? You're kidding! I have *twenty* birds!"

The clerk then asked each of us, "What'll it be?"
I looked at Sarah, and she looked at me!

Now Sarah and I, we're twin sisters at heart.
Except for one HUGE thing that sets us apart.

For me, one scoop of vanilla's just right.
For Sarah? Fudge Coconut Cherry Delight!

OK, so on ice cream we might disagree.
But really we're birds of a feather, you see.

It's odd that the moment I met her I'm sure
I saw only the wheelchair. I didn't see her.

I still think her wheelchair's a pretty neat tool,
but now I see Sarah first—and she's cool!

I'm certain if you look close that you'll also see . . .

Sarah, my best friend—a girl just like me.